Big Bad Wolfsville

Written by Timothy Knapman

Illustrated by Monica de Rivas

Collins

1 Story Town

Once upon a time, Story Town was the place where people went to live happily ever after. It was clean and tidy and no one ever did anything bad there. Princes and princesses spent their days being pampered at Rapunzel's Hair Salon. The Seven Dwarfs sang joyfully as they carried sacks of jewels from their mine to the bank for safekeeping. The bank was owned by Little Red Riding Hood's Grandma. Red visited her Grandma often, bringing treats from Hansel and Gretel's Sweet, Cake and Coffee Shop.

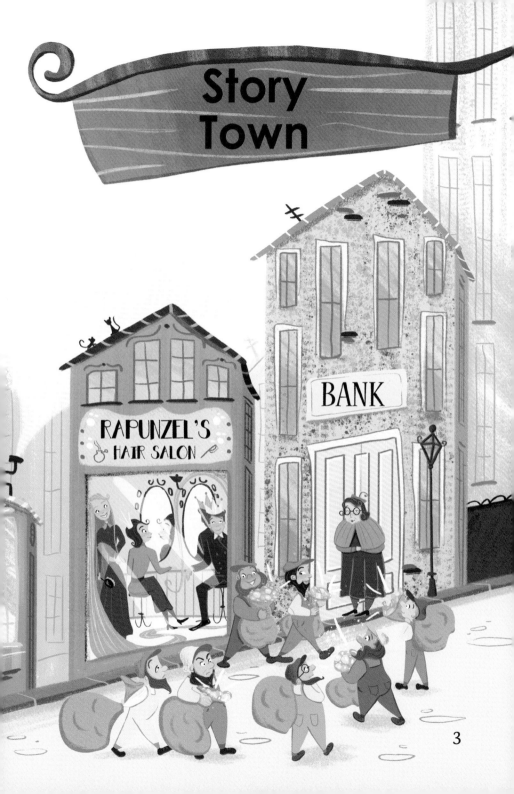

Story Town

RAPUNZEL'S HAIR SALON

BANK

Then one day, Little Bo Peep's sheep went missing.

She had let him out for a run in the park as she did every day. Only this time, he didn't come back.

Story Town only had one policeman. He was eating cake with the fairy godmothers at Hansel and Gretel's shop when Little Bo Peep burst in.

"You have to find my sheep!" she wailed. "He has the softest fleece, tied with the prettiest pink bows, and he answers to the name Teeny-Weeny Baa-Baa-kins."

The policeman was sure there was nothing to worry about. He was also sure he wanted to finish his cake in peace. "Don't worry, Miss," he chuckled, reassuringly. "This is Story Town and no one ever does anything bad here. Your sheep will come home, wagging his tail behind him."

But the sheep didn't come home, and soon other things started to go missing. First, Cinderella's glass slippers were stolen. "I don't know who could have taken them," she told the policeman. "I'm the only person they fit!"

Then Goldilocks and the Three Bears' porridge collection was burgled. "They took it all," Goldilocks told the policeman. "Too hot, too cold *and* just right!"

When someone put weedkiller on Jack's giant beanstalk, even the policeman realised that something had gone terribly wrong. Soon fear stalked the streets of Story Town. Grandma put bars on the windows of her bank. The Seven Dwarfs stopped singing and went to and from work in an armoured car.

And then the wolf came to town.

2 Big Bad Wolfsville

The streetlamps shook as a long black car came roaring into Story Town. It was driven by a hare who'd gone bad since losing a race with a tortoise and, as it screeched to a stop, it crashed right into a "No parking" sign.

The policeman took one look at the broken sign and marched over. After all the bad things that had happened, he was in no mood to be nice. "You can't do that!" he snapped.

The hare narrowed her eyes. "Take it up with the boss," she said and motioned towards the back seat. It was dark in there, and the policeman couldn't see anyone in the shadows. Then the door opened and out stepped a wolf. He was dressed in a black hat and a smart stripy suit, both a little bit too big for him.

"I'm the boss," said the wolf. "They call me ... the Big Baa-Baa-Bad Wolf."

"But you're not very big," said the policeman.

"I beg your pardon?" said the wolf in a low growl.

"I'm sure you're a wolf, and I'm sure you're bad," said the policeman, "but you don't even come up to my middle. Who's this 'they' who call you 'big'?"

The policeman realised this was the wrong thing to say when he saw the hare put her paws over her ears and disappear below the dashboard of the car. He didn't realise *how* wrong until the wolf opened his mouth.

"I ... AM ... *BIG!*" the wolf shrieked. He was so loud that the windows of nearby buildings rattled. "I am VAST! I am HUGE! I am MAAAAAASSIVE!" The wolf rolled around on the ground in his fury. He bounced up and down. He smashed things. He screamed. His tantrum was terrifying.

"All right, you're big!" said the policeman, who was very sorry he'd started this. "Now would you please stop?"

But the wolf *wouldn't* stop. Instead, he cried as loudly as he could, *"I'M THE BIG BAA-BAA-BAD WOLF!"*

It was the most horrible noise the policeman had ever heard. It got under his skin and in-between his teeth and made his ears wobble until he couldn't stand it any longer. He went running out of Story Town and was never seen again.

"Hare?" grinned the wolf.

The hare put her head above the dashboard. "Yes, boss?" she said.

"The police have gone," the wolf went on. "Now there's no one to stop us taking over this town." And they both laughed wickedly.

3 Taking over

The first thing the people of Story Town noticed was that it wasn't called "Story Town" any more. The wolf and the hare changed its name to "Big Bad Wolfsville".

Some of the braver princes tried to stop them, but the wolf threw such a scary tantrum that they ran back to their houses and hid under their beds.

Meanwhile, in their hideout – a dark old warehouse down by the docks – the wolf and the hare made their evil plans.

"Now I'm in charge, I want to be rich," said the wolf.

"We *are* rich, boss," said the hare. "We've got Cinderella's slippers and all that porridge."

"The slippers didn't fit and most of the porridge was too hot or too cold," said the wolf. "No, it's money I want, but how am I going to get it?" Then he thought about all the shops in the town. "People are always going in there to buy things so they must have lots."

Word of the wolf's terrible tantrums had spread through the town, so the shopkeepers were too scared to say no to him. He took all their money and stuffed it into a big sack.

"This sack is really heavy, boss," said the hare, who had to carry it. "How many more shops do we have to rob?"

"Stop complaining!" the wolf growled.

The rest of the shops were on the far side of a bridge which had a small hut at one end. The wolf and the hare were about to cross the bridge when a gruff little goat called Tilly stepped out of the hut.

"This is the Troll Bridge toll bridge," Tilly said. "You have to pay the toll of one gold coin before you can cross."

Troll Bridge
Toll: one gold coin

"No chance," said the wolf rudely, and he pushed past Tilly.

"Then you'll have to talk to my big sister," said Tilly, and she called out: "Milly!"

A larger, gruffer goat called Milly came out of the hut. "This is the Troll Bridge toll bridge," she said.

"And you're not getting my money!" said the wolf, pushing past Milly.

"Then you'll have to talk to my big sister," said Milly, and she called out: "Jilly!"

This time, the goat that came out of the hut was so huge and so gruff that the hare wondered how she'd ever fitted into the hut in the first place!

"Let's pay the toll, boss!" said the hare, looking up at the huge goat. "We'll still have plenty of money in the sack."

"No!" said the wolf, stamping his feet furiously. The hare could see a tantrum coming on and she didn't know who would make her more scared: the huge goat or the angry wolf.

"Then you'll have to talk to the troll who lives under the bridge," said Jilly, and she called out: "Tilly!"

"There's no such thing as trolls!" the wolf sneered, but Tilly had already disappeared under the bridge.

The wolf and the hare walked on and they were
halfway across the bridge when a loud, rumbling voice
from underneath made everything tremble.

"What did you say, Tilly?" roared the voice – so loudly
that the wolf and the hare stopped moving. "There's a
naughty wolf who won't pay the toll?! That makes me
so angry! You wait till I get my hands on him!"

The wolf looked at the hare and repeated, "There's no such thing as trolls," only this time his voice was shaking.

"No such thing as trolls?!" roared the voice. "I'll show you!"

"Eek!" squeaked the wolf. The hare dropped the sack of money and they ran back past the hut and all the way home to their hideout.

Once they'd gone, Milly and Jilly looked under the bridge to where Tilly was still holding the megaphone she'd used to make her voice sound loud and scary.

"Silly wolf," said Tilly. "Doesn't he know there's no such thing as trolls?"

And Milly, Jilly and Tilly goats gruff laughed.

4 Something very wicked

When her friends heard how Tilly had fooled
the wolf, they gathered at Hansel and Gretel's
to celebrate.

"The wolf is a bully," said Tilly, "and you have to
stand up to bullies."

"But how are we going to get rid of him?"
said Little Bo Peep. "We can't try that
rumbling voice trick again. He'll know
it's you."

Tilly had a thought. "There's something odd
about that wolf's voice. Has anyone else heard
him say that he's the 'Baa-Baa-Bad Wolf'?"

"Yes, but it's not kind to make fun of the way
people speak," said Cinderella.

"You're quite right," said Tilly. "Anyway, I'm more
worried about what the wolf is planning next.
After leaving all the stolen money behind on
the bridge, he'll want to do something very
wicked indeed."

27

Tilly was right. The wolf had come up with a very wicked plan. That afternoon, he and the hare were hiding outside the Seven Dwarfs' mine. They watched as the Dwarfs came out, carrying sacks filled with jewels. The wolf and the hare waited until the Dwarfs had put the sacks into their armoured car, and then pounced.

"I'll keep this short, Dwarfs," said the wolf. "The hare and I are going to steal your jewels, and your armoured car. If you make any fuss, I'll throw a tantrum."

"Take the jewels! Take the car!" said the Dwarfs, sounding very afraid.

The wolf and the hare hooted with laughter as they clambered aboard the armoured car.

"Where to, boss?" asked the hare. "Home to our hideout?"

"No," said the wolf, "we're going to Grandma's bank. When we arrive in this armoured car, she'll think we're the Dwarfs bringing jewels to her for safekeeping and she'll let us in. Then we can steal everything in the bank!"

"Brilliant idea, boss!" cackled the hare.

The moment the armoured car pulled up outside
the bank, Grandma opened the doors. The wolf and
the hare ran in. Grandma couldn't see very well so
she took off her glasses and peered closely at them.

"You're not the Seven Dwarfs!" she said in an old lady voice.

"No, we're not!" grinned the wolf. "Now give us everything or I'll throw the biggest tantrum ever!"

"Aren't you a little bit old for tantrums?" asked Grandma, but she wasn't speaking in an old lady voice any more. The wolf looked closely at her.

"Grandma, what big horns you have," he said.

"All the better to stop your wicked plan," said Tilly, who was only pretending to be Grandma!

"You're that wretched goat!" said the wolf.

"Yes," said Tilly, "and this is a trap!
Come out, everyone!"

From their hiding places in the bank, the goats, fairy godmothers, princes, princesses and all of Tilly's other friends and neighbours stood up.

"Bad luck, Mr Wolf," said Tilly. "We've got you surrounded."

"Sorry, boss!" shrieked the hare. "But I'm only doing this for the money." She grabbed one of the sacks of jewels from the car and ran off.

"Come back, you coward!" yelled the wolf, but the hare was already too far away to hear.

"Don't worry," said Tilly. "She'll soon realise that the jewels in that sack are just boiled sweets from Hansel and Gretel's. It's over and you've lost."

"Lost?" growled the wolf. "ME?" Everyone could see that the wolf was building up to the biggest tantrum ever. "DON'T YOU KNOW WHO I AM?" The noise was so horrible that all of Tilly's friends and neighbours ran away. Tilly knew he was a bully, and that you had to stand up to bullies, but she was still quite scared of him. "I am the BIG ... BAA-BAA-BAD ... WOLF!"

And then Tilly noticed something, and she wasn't so scared after all.

5 All the better

Tilly goat gruff was all alone with the big bad wolf
in Grandma's bank. The wolf was very cross, and it
looked like he was going to throw the biggest tantrum
ever, but Tilly wasn't afraid. She even started to smile.

"Oh, Mr Wolf," she said, "what big ears you have!"

"All the better to – " said the wolf, but before he could finish speaking, Tilly leant forward and grabbed one of his ears. It came off in her hand. So did his other ear, and his nose, his claws …

"What are you doing?" cried the wolf. "Don't you know who I am? I'm the Big Baa-Baa – "

"I *do* know who you are – *and* why you call yourself the Baa-Baa-Bad Wolf," said Tilly, as she pulled off more of the disguise the wolf had been wearing all this time.

"You aren't a wolf at all," said Tilly. "You are Teeny-Weeny Baa-Baa-kins, Little Bo Peep's runaway sheep!"

"Don't call me that," said the sheep. "I am big and baa-baa-bad!"

But Tilly had already called Little Bo Peep, who came rushing in and grabbed her sheep. "My cuddly-wuddly little Teeny-Weeny Baa-Baa-kins, you've come home!" she said, covering him with sloppy kisses.

"Could somebody PLEASE send me to prison?" said the sheep.

But the sheep in wolf's clothing wasn't sent to prison. Instead, his fleece was shampooed until it was soft and fluffy, and he was once again tied with pretty bows so he couldn't throw any more tantrums. The sheep hated it, but Little Bo Peep made sure he never ran off again.

Big Bad Wolfsville went back to being Story Town, and Tilly, her sisters and all her friends and neighbours went back to doing what they liked best: living happily ever after.

Police report

The "wolf"

A desperate criminal who will stop at nothing to make himself rich.

Likes: money, everyone doing what he says, naming things after himself

Doesn't like: people saying no to him, Bo Peep, pink bows

Special power: tantrums

Tilly

A goat who runs the Troll Bridge toll bridge with her two sisters.

Likes: living happily ever after, her sisters

Doesn't like: bullies, people who don't pay the toll

Special power: fooling bad people, doing the right thing even when she's scared

The hare

A hare who once lost a race to a tortoise and never forgave herself.

Likes: winning races, eating porridge with a glass slipper

Doesn't like: going slowly, tortoises, stealing from people who make a fuss

Special power: driving

The policeman

He came to crime-free Story Town for an easy life, but it didn't work out.

Likes: cake, people being nice to each other

Doesn't like: bad people, anything that interrupts cake time

Special power: anything to do with cake

Ideas for reading

Written by Clare Dowdall, PhD
Lecturer and Primary Literacy Consultant

Reading objectives:
- discuss the sequence of events in books and how items of information are related
- become increasingly familiar with and retell a wider range of stories, fairy stories and traditional tales
- make inferences on the basis of what is being said and done
- predict what might happen on the basis of what has been read so far

Spoken language objectives:
- use spoken language to develop understanding through speculating, hypothesising, imagining and exploring ideas
- participate in discussions, presentations, performances and debates

Curriculum links: PSHE – health and wellbeing; Writing – composition

Word count: 2512

Interest words: pampered, fear stalked the streets, sheep in wolf's clothing, tantrum

Resources: ICT or paper and pencils to prepare a police report, large sheets of paper, whiteboards

Build a context for reading

- Look at the front cover and read the title, then discuss what the words *Big Bad Wolfsville* mean. Check children understand that Wolfsville is a place.
- Ask children to talk about the fairy tales that they know with wolves in. Do the children think that it is fair that wolves are usually made out to be "big and bad" in stories?
- Read the blurb to the children and ask them to suggest which fairy-tale character might stand up to the Big Bad Wolf in this story, and what they might do.

Understand and apply reading strategies

- Ask for a volunteer to read the introduction to the story on page 2. Challenge children to predict which other fairy-tale characters might live in Story Town, and what they might like to do there.
- Continue to read Chapter 1 as a group. Dwell on the sentence *"Soon fear stalked the streets of Story Town."* (p7). Ask children to consider